To my parents, and my brother and sister
—E. H.

Henry Holt and Company, Inc.
Publishers since 1866
115 West 18th Street
New York, New York 10011

Henry Holt is a registered trademark of Henry Holt and Company, Inc.
Text copyright © 1995 by Tim Chadwick.
Illustrations copyright © 1995 by Emma Harding. All rights reserved.
First published in the United States in 1995 by
Henry Holt and Company, Inc.
Published in Canada by Fitzhenry & Whiteside Ltd.,
195 Allstate Parkway, Markham, Ontario L3R 4T8.
Originally published in the United Kingdom in 1995 by
ABC (All Books for Children), a division of
The All Children's Company Ltd., London.

Library of Congress Cataloging-in-Publication Data
The Headless Horseman: a retelling of The legend of
Sleepy Hollow/by Washington Irving: illustrated by
Emma Harding.
Summary: A superstitious schoolmaster, in love
with a wealthy farmer's daughter, has a terrifying
encounter with a headless horseman.
[1. Ghosts—Fiction, 2. New York (State)—Fiction.]   I. Harding,
Emma, ill.   II. Irving, Washington, 1783–1859.   Legend of Sleepy Hollow.
PZ7.H3423   1994   [E]—dc20   94-10276

ISBN 0-8050-3584-2
First American Edition—1995
Printed in Hong Kong.

1   3   5   7   9   10   8   6   4   2

The artist used oil paints on handmade hemoline paper
to create the illustrations for this book.

THE HEADLESS HORSEMAN

A Retelling of Washington Irving's

"The Legend of Sleepy Hollow"

illustrated by Emma Harding

———

Henry Holt and Company • New York

Not far from a broad expanse of the Hudson River there is a peaceful little wooded valley called Sleepy Hollow. Many years ago its inhabitants, who were not only skilled farmers but imaginative storytellers, would tell of strange apparitions, and of music and voices in the night. A dreamy, magical spell seemed to hang over this beautiful glen, and every traveler who passed through it felt its bewitching power.

In those days, the schoolmaster in Sleepy Hollow was called Ichabod Crane. His name fit him well: he was tall and thin with long arms and legs, and feet like shovels. When he loped along on his way to school, the children said he looked like a scarecrow escaped from a field.

The country folk—especially
the ladies—enjoyed entertaining
the schoolmaster. He loved to
gossip and to hear the marvelous
local tales of haunted brooks and
bridges, and ghosts and goblins.
The most legendary of these
tales was that of the Headless
Horseman, who some claimed
to have seen riding through the
valley at midnight. The stories
would gather in Ichabod's head
as he walked home at dusk,
when every sound and shadow
made him tremble and cringe.

Tales of the supernatural were one of the three great loves of Ichabod's life. The other two were food, which he consumed in mountainous quantities, and Katrina, the plump and beautiful daughter of Old Van Tassel, a wealthy farmer. But alas, Katrina's beauty, charm, and wealth were known far and wide, and many men sought her affections.

One warm autumn evening, Van Tassel invited all of Sleepy Hollow to celebrate his abundant harvest. To the delight of his students, Ichabod Crane closed school early that day in order to dress and prepare for the evening.

As he rode Gunpowder, an old but fiery horse, to Van Tassel's farm, Ichabod's head filled with thoughts of delectable foods and the lovely heiress.

Ichabod was not disappointed when he
arrived. The tables groaned under the weight
of roasted meats, pies and cakes, and preserves
of every fruit.

After he had feasted, the loose-limbed schoolmaster showed off his dancing skills as he waltzed Katrina around the room to the admiration of all—except Ichabod's main rival for Katrina's affections, Brom Van Brunt.

Brom Van Brunt was a young man of enormous strength and herculean stature, which earned him the nickname Brom Bones. His skill as a horseman was unsurpassed, and he and his companions would often be heard at night, thundering along the lanes, playing mischievous pranks on the country folk.

After the dance, Ichabod joined some of the men who were smoking their pipes and gossiping quietly. When the talk turned to tales of ghosts and goblins, Brom Bones told of his recent encounter with the Headless Horseman. The ghost had pursued him through the woods, but the skilled Bones and his flashing steed had outrun him. According to local lore, if you could reach the bridge at the end of the valley before the Headless Horseman did, the apparition would disappear. Sure enough, as Bones's horse had touched the wooden planks of the bridge, his hellish pursuer was consumed in a flash of fire and vanished.

The assembled group shivered with terror at the thought of this midnight adventure.

As the evening drew to a close, Ichabod Crane lingered behind to speak with Katrina. After a few moments, he suddenly turned and, without a word, marched out of the house looking crestfallen.

Deep in thought, he rode into the night. The stars appeared to be drawn back into the heavens and clouds passed across the moon. The woods seemed to close about him with inky blackness. An old gnarled tulip tree moaned as its branches rubbed together in the chilly night breeze. As Ichabod approached the stream, he heard a faint splash. Gunpowder froze.

Peering out across the stream,
Ichabod thought he saw a huge
horseman standing silently
in the shadow of the trees.
He called out, "Who are
you?" but received no reply.
With his heart thumping
wildly, he turned Gunpowder
to the road and kicked him hard.

The old horse jolted away but there were now
hoofbeats close behind him. Crane turned and caught
his breath in horror at the figure outlined in the faint
moonlight. It was gigantic in height, muffled in a
cloak—and headless. Even more horrible, its head
appeared to be stuck to the pommel of the saddle.

With a desperate flurry of kicks and whips,
Crane flung Gunpowder into a gallop. The old
horse careened in panic down the dark lane.

The schoolmaster felt the hot breath of the terrible horse behind him as he rode for his life. His saddle slipped beneath him and fell into the road. Ahead in the gloom Crane could just make out the white shape of the church and he knew that the bridge was near. "If only I can make that bridge, I'm safe," he thought, and hurled Gunpowder into the darkness.

Suddenly the horse's hooves touched the first planks of the bridge and he was across it in a flash. Ichabod Crane turned to make sure that the specter had stopped. Instead, he saw that the grotesque horseman was in the act of hurling his head directly at him and, before Ichabod Crane could duck, it hit him with a sickly crash on the forehead.

The next day the townspeople found Gunpowder walking alone and saddleless in a field. Ichabod Crane's hat was discovered on the slope next to the bridge and, near it, a shattered pumpkin. The schoolmaster was never seen again.

The people of Sleepy Hollow talked for years of this strange incident. Some assumed that he had left, heartbroken, after his rejection by Katrina. Others said that he'd left to study law, and became a politician. Most maintained that Ichabod Crane had been carried off to Hades by the Headless Horseman.

Soon after the unfortunate incident, Brom Bones took the lovely Katrina for his wife.

Often the story of the Headless Horseman
would be retold around the fire on winter
evenings. And whenever the broken pumpkin
was mentioned, Bones would give a knowing
wink and chuckle to himself.